Shine

SCHOLASTIC

Dedicated to my nephews and nieces – always let your light shine.

With thanks to my parents – your sacrifices and love will forever be appreciated.

S. A.

Published by Scholastic in the UK, 2023
1 London Bridge, London, SE1 9BG
Scholastic Ireland, 89E Lagan Road, Dublin Industrial Estate, Glasnevin, Dublin, D11 HP5F

ISBN 978 07023 2487 1

A CIP catalogue record for this book is available from the British Library.

Printed and bound in China
Paper made from wood grown in sustainable forests and other controlled sources.

13 5 7 9 10 8 6 4 2

www.scholastic.co.uk

Shine

Sarah Asuquo

Illustrated by
Nadia Fisher

SCHOLASTIC

"Bye, Mum!"

yelled Kai as he raced briskly towards the school gates. It was the first day of school after the summer holiday and Kai could not wait to see his friends.

But, Kai's journey home was very different
to the cheerful ride in the morning.

"How was your day, Kai?"
his mother asked. Kai, sighed
deeply, and replied,

"We built a den at school today,
for kids to hide, explore and play.
I thought the den was built for all,
but they said, 'No, Kai. You're too tall.'

I wish that I was smaller.
I wish I wasn't tall.
Then I could fit inside the den
like Tom and Anne and Paul."

"Be proud, my son, that you are tall; stand as high as you can be.
For you can see far beyond what other children see.
Everyone is different, son. You must be true to you.
Within us all is a special light.
Will you let yours shine through?"

Kai simply nodded.

The following night at bedtime,
Kai's parents saw that he was upset again.

"At lunchtime in the dining hall,
while eating apple pie,
Jack pointed and then asked me,
'What's that under your eye?'
'It's just a scar,' I told him,
'I fell when I was small.'

He laughed and said, **'That's strange,'**
and led the laughter in the hall.
I wish that I was perfect,
I wish I had no scars.
Then I'd be like my friends at school.
I'd be normal like they are."

With a calm voice, Kai's father said,

"Be proud, my son, of all your scars,
don't be ashamed or hide.
They show you've learned and overcome,
they add to your own shine."

He pulled open Kai's curtains, revealing the bright night sky.

"Look up at the stars at night – they **twinkle** in the sky.

Then watch the **moonlight** up above the clouds, so very high.

Can you compare the stars and moon and say that one is **best?**

They both **shine** in the sky each night so beautifully as we rest.

Everyone is different, son. You must be true to you.
Within us all is a special light. Will you let yours shine through?"

Kai firmly nodded as his parents tucked him into bed,
kissed his forehead and wished him a good night.

Kai realized that the things that make him different are the things that make him special.

"I choose to use all the things that make me who I am, and make sure that I **shine** my light as brightly as I can."

The next day at playtime, Kai's friend, Sam, was very sad.

"I went out to the playground to play basketball,
but everybody laughed at me; Jack said I was too small.

I wish that I was taller. I wish I was like you.
Then I could hop and leap and jump, just like the others do."

Kai told Sam what he had learned about the stars and the moon.

"You can Shine your special light just the way you are.
You move so quickly when you play, just like a shooting star.
With my height and your speed, we'll make a perfect team.

I've got a great idea, Sam...

...you can play with me!"

Kai leaped and jumped,
shooting the ball through the hoop,
while Sam sped across the playground,
bouncing the ball with great skill.

The children in their class
watched them and
cheered.

Jack realized that he had been unkind.

"Hi, Kai and Sam. I watched the game, you both play really well.
I'm sorry that I laughed at you ... may I play as well?"

Kai and Sam looked at each other and
smiled with great delight...

"Of course," said Kai,
"we all can **Shine**
if we just unite."

Questions to help you SHINE

When Kai and Sam are teased for being different, they wish that they were like other children instead. Why should we try not to compare ourselves to others?

Kai's dad explains to him how the moon and the stars can both shine beautifully, side by side. How does this help to show that people who are different can both shine?

When Jack realized that he had been mean to Kai and Sam, he said sorry. When should we say we're sorry to others? Why is it important to do this?

Kai and Sam were happy to accept Jack's apology and let him play with them. Is it important to forgive others? Why?